THE WEE SCOTCH PIPER

MADELINE BRANDEIS

Edition : Culturea (Hérault, 34)
Contact : infos@culturea.fr
Print in Germany by Books on Demand
Design and layout : Derek Murphy
Layout : Reedsy (https://reedsy.com/)
ISBN : 9791041828784
Légal deposit : July 2023

The Wee Scotch Piper

CHAPTER I

THE CRAIG FAMILY

In the wee village of Aberfoyle, which is in Perthshire County, Scotland, lived Alan Craig, a shepherd.

The sheep of Scotland, like the bagpipes and bluebells, are famous, and in Aberfoyle there are many.

Dotted alongside the road are the bright bluebells, lighting up in true fairy array the darkness made by big, shady trees.

Shrieking through the stillness of a summer evening, comes the sound of the bagpipes. This music is furnished by a tattered piper marching up and down, up and down. He hopes that the people will throw pennies for the love of the tune he plays.

And the sheep, like little dots of white in the green meadows, graze. But sometimes, they, too, shriek when they are herded together, perhaps for the clipping.

When the sheep all bleat together, it sounds very much like the shrieking of the bagpipes. Maybe that is how the bagpipe was really started. Perhaps the sound was first uttered by a herd of Scotch sheep!

It was not yet clipping time on the small farm of Alan Craig. His sheep still roamed the hills. Their heavy, curly wool weighed them down and made them look as if they had on long, woollen nighties.

The babies sometimes walked right under their mothers, and then they were completely hidden.

On a hill sat Alan Craig, and by his side his faithful dog, Roy. Roy was a real sheep dog and was proud of his profession.

You know, when people are called professionals, it means that they are trained in one occupation. Of course, people make money at their professions, and this was the only difference between Roy and a professional human.

Roy was a professional sheep dog, but he did his work out of devotion to his master. Also he did it because it was in his blood to love to race the timid sheep over the hills and obey his master's commands.

"Back, Roy!" shouted Alan Craig.

Roy jumped to his feet and, barking, ran to bring back the flock, which had disappeared around a rocky mountain.

"Bowwow-wow!" The sheep heard him coming and, stupid creatures that they are, started to run the other way. "Bowwow!"

"Down, sir, down!" came the voice of Alan Craig from afar, and Roy understood.

Silently he made a dash for the leading sheep and, bounding ahead of the herd, he stood on guard. His feet were planted apart, and his tongue hung out. He was barking in his own language a short Scotch bark, which meant, "Now, will you go back?"

All but the leading sheep began to turn. That leader was, however, a mother sheep with a loved baby. She had always been very suspicious of Roy.

Perhaps he had once snapped at her baby, for he often had to do this to make the sheep behave. At any rate, the mother sheep could not forgive him. Without any fear, she now sprang toward Roy and butted her head in defiance.

Roy stood his ground and then made a plunge at her legs. Meanwhile, he let out a shrill bark as one of her sharp horns hit his leg. It was a short but hard battle.

At last Roy returned to his master, his tongue nearly sweeping the ground. But there was a triumphant expression in his eyes as he drove the crowd of panting sheep into a circle around Alan Craig and threw himself at his master's feet to await his reward.

This was not long in coming. Alan Craig appreciated his helper. In fact Roy was really the shepherd. Alan had only to speak his commands—"work his dog," as the Scotch say—and Roy did the rest.

Now he stroked his dog and said, "Good, Roy! Well done!"

Alan's language was well understood by Roy, but these words would have sounded this way to you: "Gude, Roy! Weel dune!" had Alan spoken in the Scotch dialect to Roy.

He could speak very good English, and did when he spoke to Englishmen. But you see, Roy was a Scotchman!

From the little white cottage in the hollow came the smell of dinner—fresh pancakes and meat cooking.

Alan picked up his crook—the kind that little Bopeep used—only Alan did not look like little Bopeep. Indeed, he was very different.

He was a big strong man. Although we picture a Scotch shepherd dressed in kilts and socks and perhaps a tam, Alan Craig wore none of these. Kilts and socks and tams are for the gentry, Alan would tell you, and shepherds are too poor to afford them.

So Alan wore an old suit which might have once been worn by your own father and then given away to some beggar. Alan was poor like most of the villagers, for Scotland is rather a poor country.

Still, in the little village of Aberfoyle, everyone was happy. In the evenings the people from the big city of Glasgow came in big buses. They danced outside on the village green to the tune of the pipes, while they gloried in the fresh country air.

So you must not think that Alan Craig and his family suffered. Indeed, there could hardly have been a happier little family in Scotland.

That evening Alan wended his way homeward and was met by his wife and baby. If you have ever seen how an Indian mother carries her baby, then you will know how Mrs. Craig carried hers. Only instead of carrying it on her back as the Indians do, she carried it in front wrapped securely in her plaid shawl.

Her one arm was thus free, and she worked most of the day this way, while knowing and feeling her little one safe in her arms.

The family sat down to dinner in their wee kitchen, for the farmers have no such luxury as a dining room. They started their soup, a thick broth made of barley and vegetables of all kinds. Mother Craig poured it out of the big tureen.

Just at this time, the door burst open, and a ruddy-faced boy of ten years rushed into the room.

"Ian Craig, do you know the hour?" asked Mother Craig.

The boy stood in the doorway and smiled at the family. He sniffed with delight the pleasant odor coming to him from the table.

"Ay, Mother," answered the boy. "Well do I know."

Then he prepared to take his place at the table, with a gesture of rubbing his stomach in thinking of what was to be put inside.

"What a bonny smell, Mother!" he continued. "And surely the taste is even bonnier!"

"'Tis the glib tongue you have, Ian Craig," laughed his father. "You could write poetry to the smell of a good dinner! And now, what have you to tell us to-night?"

Now, Ian was always full of stories and tales of adventure. He was one of those children to whom something exciting is always happening.

So the family were quite accustomed to having him return home with vivid tales. Some were strange, some droll and, alas, some sad and painful, told to the tune of bandages and arnica.

Still, what boy is not sometimes hurt? And Ian's accidents were few, in comparison to his other experiences. Surely, it is to be wondered how, in a small, quiet town like Aberfoyle, so many wondrous happenings could occur.

Sometimes Ian was doubted, not, however, by his parents, who knew that their son was truthful. The schoolmaster knew it, too, and was proud of Ian, whose stories and poems were the best in his class.

One day he was recounting to a group of spellbound school children his experiences of the day. He was relating what wondrous happenings had befallen him, when he was interrupted by a boy who shouted, "Ian Craig is telling lies!"

The boy was a year older than Ian, but he was never known to make sport of Ian again. Nor did Ian ever admit to his parents how it happened that he arrived home from school that day with a swollen eye.

CHAPTER II

SANDY'S FIRST VISIT

Aberfoyle is the center of the "Rob Roy country." Rob Roy MacGregor was, as every child knows, a great Scotch warrior and represented one of the oldest Highland clans.

In Aberfoyle, where Ian Craig lived, stands the old house in which Sir Walter Scott wrote his famous story "Rob Roy." To-day it houses the village minister.

Near by is a tumble-down thatched cottage known as "Jean McAlpin's Inn," where Rob Roy was wont to rest.

A landmark in the village is the old "Rob Roy Brig." Here on the old brig (which means "bridge" in Scotch) Ian would sit when school was out and his chores at home were finished.

Something usually happened when he sat here, and many of his experiences had started from this bridge. Often, while he waited for adventure, Ian fished from the bridge. He brought home fine, fat morsels, for the river Forth, which flows beneath the bridge, is rich in fish.

But Ian's dearest memory was of Sandy. The Sandy adventure had taken place almost a year before, but it was as vivid in Ian's mind as though it had all occurred the day before.

It happened while Ian was fishing from the brig. He heard the sound of bagpipes—a sound that is nothing unusual to hear in Scotland. Still it always made Ian joyous and sad at once. And now he turned to listen.

This playing was the loveliest he had ever heard. Jamie Robinson played almost every night in front of the old hotel, and Ian loved the music. But this playing was different. He had always thought Jamie's playing good, but he now wondered how he could ever have thought so.

This tune was from far away, but it carried across the meadow and along the road. And then he saw Sandy! Sandy was standing still in the middle of the road while he played.

By his side was a handcart, and Ian knew at once what it meant. Sandy was a wandering piper, a man who has no home, a gypsy. He piped for his living and camped on the road.

Many pipers passed through Aberfoyle, some with large families. In fact, Jamie was one of them, only Jamie did not travel. He lived in the woods near Aberfoyle in a tent with his wife and babies.

But no one had ever played like this before. Ian ran up the road. As he approached the newcomer, he could see that the piper was a little old man.

He had a kindly, wrinkled face, and twinkling eyes which winked at Ian as the boy came closer. Then suddenly he changed his tune.

"Bonny laddie, Highland laddie," shrieked the pipes.

Ian stopped in front of the piper and thought he should cry. The music ceased.

A hand was laid on Ian's shoulder, and a voice asked, "And why, laddie, do you stand and look with eyes so big and sad?"

Ian then realized that he had been staring as if in a trance. He brought himself back to earth, smiled, and put out his hand.

"I'm sorry, sir. I was only admiring your bonny piping!"

"Ach!" laughed the piper. "And I was only admiring the bonny laddie! What's your name?"

"Ian Craig."

"And mine's Sandy. You may call me Sandy, though my name's really Evert Robert MacKeith MacGregor, and my great-grandfather was a cousin to the great Rob Roy."

With these words, Sandy MacGregor put his pipes into his cart. Then, slinging the rope over his shoulders, he started to pull his load along, while Ian kept step with him.

"And a fine village this is—the scene of my ancestor's home! Do you live here, my lad?"

"Ay, Sandy, and not far from old Rob Roy Brig."

"Well, well," sighed Sandy. "And could we bide a wee on the old brig of my ancestor while Sandy rests?"

"Ay, could we," said Ian with great delight, "and I can pull your cart for you, Sandy, until we get there."

Gratefully the old man allowed the boy to pull his load, while he stretched his tired arms. He breathed in the sweet-smelling air of the village of his ancestor.

When they came to the bridge, Ian put down the cart. He invited Sandy to sit beside him on the wall, his usual perch. The old man jumped up to the boy's side, as spry as the boy himself, and looked around.

"Well, well," he said, "and to think 'tis Sandy's first visit to the home of his ancestor—Sandy who has been nigh all over the land!"

At these words Ian's heart gave a bound, and he said, "Have you seen nigh all of bonny Scotland, Sandy?"

"Ay, that have I, lad, and traveled on my own two feet through it all."

"Sandy," said Ian wistfully, "would you be telling me about it?"

"Ach, ay, laddie," smiled the old wanderer. "That would I, for 'tis many a fine sight these old eyes have seen."

Sandy talked, and the boy listened. The sun grew lower and lower in the heavens. Ian Craig thought that never before had he known an afternoon to slip by so quickly.

Sandy told Ian about the time he had visited Edinburgh, Scotland's capital, and one of the most attractive cities in the world.

He told of Princes Street, with its sunken gardens on one side, and its wonderful view of historic Edinburgh Castle, its pretty shops and stately monuments. It is considered by many to be the most beautiful street in all the world.

On the top of a winding hill is Edinburgh Castle. Here, in the courtyard of the old castle is Half-Moon Battery, where is kept the one-o'clock gun.

This gun fires every day at the hour of one. It is attached by electric wire to the time ball on the top of Nelson's Monument on Carlton Hill opposite. This ball falls, in turn, at a signal from Greenwich Observatory, near London, where is set the time for the whole world.

In another part of the castle grounds can be found a pathetic little plot of ground known as "The Dogs' Cemetery." Here are buried the pets of the soldiers who fought in the World War.

Many of these little beasts were gallant heroes and were buried with great reverence. Lovely flowers decorate their graves, and inscriptions tell of each one's valor.

But to one little dog in particular was a fountain erected. It stands in one of the streets of Edinburgh. This fountain represents "Greyfriars' Bobby," as the little dog was called.

He was given this name because it was to the old Greyfriars Churchyard that he went, day after day, to seek his master, who was buried there. The caretakers of the cemetery tried to keep him out.

Still day after day he came. He always lay upon the grave of his master and grieved, until one day they found him dead. And now the fountain is there to remind the people of this faithful little creature.

CHAPTER III

PIPERS

"Do you think my dog would grieve if I should die?" asked Ian, as he brushed away a tear with his sleeve and tried to distract Sandy's attention from his action.

"Ay, if you treat him kindly, lad," answered the old man. "Beasties are faithful to us when they know we love them."

"Ay," said Ian. "Roy is faithful, and a smart sheep dog, too."

"Do you like fine to herd the sheep, laddie?" asked Sandy.

Ian hung his head.

"No, Sandy. I like finer to go about and have adventures and make up that I am—" He hesitated.

"What, lad? Speak. Do not be afraid of Sandy for he knows the hearts of laddies well."

"If I could play the pipes, Sandy, I would go away and be a piper in the band some day," confessed Ian.

This was, indeed, a dream so near to his heart that he had never before spoken it aloud. After the admission, Ian turned his head away and did not look at Sandy. But the old man's voice was very soft and his tone caressing, as he said, "And a fine dream it is, Ian lad, for to be a piper is a great and honored calling."

"Ay," answered Ian huskily, "but 'tis not for me, Sandy."

Sandy turned the boy around then and looked him squarely in the eye.

"Ian, lad, do not speak so, for nothing is too hard to get when you want it."

Ian's eyes lighted up for a moment. Then the same forlorn look came into them as he let his head droop.

"No, Sandy. The pipes are too dear, and it takes many months to learn to play."

"And you study hard at school, lad?" asked the piper.

"Ay, do I," spoke the boy.

"Then some day, you'll be liking to hear of the fine military school I saw."

"Ach, Sandy, tell me about it. Have you really seen it?" Ian was at once alert.

"Ay, that have I, and only three weeks ago when I was passing by Dunblane."

As the poor little village lad drank in his words, Sandy talked on about the wonderful school in Dunblane. This school is called the Queen Victoria School. Here lads between the ages of nine and fifteen are trained as soldiers.

They are sons of military men, some of whom fell in the World War. These boys are reared and taught free of charge. It is a great and good school for a boy to attend.

To see and hear these sons of Scotland's heroes is an experience never to be forgotten. They present a fine appearance in their bright-colored kilts and military trappings, as they march and play upon their pipes.

Sandy saw and heard, and carried away with him a memory of the loveliest sight and sound imaginable. Coming toward him were boys. Children they were, with their kilts making a vivid pattern.

Their bare knees moved in perfect unison as they stepped to the tunes of Scotland's patriotic melodies. They played in a way unsurpassed by pipers older and more experienced than they.

First came a waltz, gracefully played and gracefully stepped. Then came a march, loud, fast, but always in perfect harmony. The sound might have come from a single organ played, perhaps, by Scottish cherubim.

The drum major wore a plumed helmet and carried a baton. He was only fourteen years old, but he twirled his stick and marched like a veteran of many wars.

The little twelve-year-old drummer swung his drumsticks into the air and caught them again. He never missed a beat on his drum. The rest, pipers all, marched and played. Their cheeks puffed in and out, while their fingers moved and made melodies.

Throughout the hills echoed the sound. It was the same as echoed during the Battle of Bannockburn, when Scottish history was made. To these tunes, in this same rugged country marched, years ago, these lads' ancestors.

And Sandy carried his memories of Queen Victoria School back to Ian Craig. Ian's longing to become a piper grew greater as he listened. In his heart he uttered a silent prayer.

CHAPTER IV

SANDY RETURNS

Though his meeting with Sandy had happened many months before, neither the memory of Sandy nor of the pipers had dimmed in Ian's mind. Through his hours of work and play his thoughts turned to marching Highland laddies and shrieking pipes.

He would often imagine himself as one of their number. Indeed, often on his walks to school he would "make believe," as so many children call it. People would turn to see why the little boy in kilts marched so straight and puffed his cheeks out.

Ian wore kilts, though his father did not. Many of the children went to school in their kilts. Yet many could not afford to do this and wore them only on Sundays.

Ian, however, had a school kilt and a Sunday kilt and was very proud of his wardrobe. One of the main reasons for his pride lay in the fact that in kilts he could better imagine himself a piper.

Marching alone one morning, he met Elsie. Elsie was only a wee lass, far younger than Ian. But she liked the tall boy who always smiled at her and who walked so straight.

Ian liked Elsie better than the other lassies, who did not understand, as Elsie did, the importance and grandeur of pipers. Besides, the others were either too freckled, or their cheeks too red.

Some Scotch children have the complexions of bright sunsets. Ian liked Elsie's bonny face, with the few little freckles on her nose, and her sunny smile.

This morning Elsie overtook him as he was marching to his own silent drone of pipes.

"Do not march so, Ian. The children will be laughing at you when you reach the school. I heard them saying you're daft about pipers, and I thought I'd tell you," she said.

Ian looked down into the little maiden's blue eyes. She, too, was dressed in a kilt. She wore over it a red jersey.

Unlike Ian, she did not have the sporran. That is what the Scotch call the piece of fur hanging down in front of the kilt. Each child's kilt was, however, pinned on the side with a large safety pin—which is the style in wearing kilts.

Elsie's hair was done in two braids, which hung down her back. Though he resented what she told him, Ian thought she was very sweet. For she looked at him in a way that made his resentment soon fade.

Smiling, he said, "Thanks, Elsie. I'll not march now."

Silently they walked together. Ian was very near telling his little friend about his dreams.

But while he was weighing the probable outcome of such a move, the school bell rang. It was half past nine, the time that school in Scotland starts in the springtime. Ian and Elsie ran.

At one o'clock, Ian went home to his lunch. Elsie stayed, for her home was far away. She brought her "piece," which is what the Scotch children call their lunch. No doubt the word refers to their piece of bread, which, with an apple, is sometimes all they get.

At home, Ian's mother always had waiting for him a plate of Scotch broth, potatoes, and sometimes an apple tart. After school Ian was drawn to the bridge.

The work at home was not pressing to-day. Father was away with the sheep. Mother did not need Ian. His heart was light as he started off for the old brig. He walked along with the hope of adventure, while in his ears the imaginary sound of pipes played.

"Ian, wait," called Elsie, and ran after him.

Ian stopped and remembered that he had almost told her. How could a wee lass like that understand? No. He would not speak. What was more, he would not let her come along, for he knew that was what she wanted to do.

"Are you going fishing from the brig?" asked Elsie blithely.

"Ay," answered Ian sulkily, as he stepped ahead of her.

"May I go with you, Ian?" queried the small girl.

"No, Elsie. You're too wee for fishing, and you scare the fish."

Elsie's lip quivered. Ian feared she would cry right out on the road. Then what would he do?

"Ach, don't cry, lass. Run home to your mother, for 'tis late for you to be out, and she'll be worried."

It was all said kindly but much too eagerly. Elsie, who was keen, did not doubt for a moment that she was not wanted.

She ran off, while Ian, with a sigh—sad to say, of relief—ran to his home. He kissed his mother, took down his fishing rod, and was off for fish and dreams.

At the bridge, adventure indeed awaited him, had he but known. He settled himself in his favorite place and threw his line down into the river. Little did he suspect what was to happen.

Singing to himself, he waited. A tug on his line! So soon? Ah, the fish were biting well to-day. Mother would be pleased. What a big fish and how it pulled! Ian struggled for several minutes, and then up came his prize.

But what sort of fish was this? It looked like a fuzzy ball of brown fur. As it came up closer, Ian saw that it was a bear—a toy bear. It was undoubtedly the property of a certain Elsie Campbell!

"Out, you wee devil, out!" cried Ian, standing up and looking down under the bridge for his tormentor.

There she was, and her laugh was most annoying to Ian. He was scolding, and at the same time trying to undo the hook from the toy bear's fur.

"Come up here, you wee devil!" repeated Ian furiously.

Up came the culprit. Ian had to join in her laughter, though he shook his finger at her the while. She sat down beside him happily.

"Ian, do you believe in the devil?" she asked.

"Ay, do I," he answered. "'Tis yerself."

"No." Elsie shook her head seriously. "Do you know, I believe 'tis like Santa Claus. 'Tis your own father!"

"Ach, Elsie," laughed Ian, at the child's idea. "You know that Santa Claus brings you dolls and toy bears and—"

Ian did not go on to complete the list, for just then he heard a sound that made his heart beat faster. Jumping down from the wall, he looked up the road. Coming toward him was Sandy!

How Elsie ever disappeared Ian never knew. Disappear she did quickly. Afterwards, when Ian thought it over, it seemed that fairies had snatched her away.

Whatever happened, she was not there when Sandy and Ian greeted each other. It was probably her woman's instinct, which bade her leave these two to their men's affairs!

SANDY ARRIVES

How happy was Ian as his kind old friend seated himself by Ian's side with the same boyish leap!

"Well, Ian, lad," said Sandy, "the same bonny Aberfoyle, the same bonny laddie! And do you have the same bonny dreams?"

"Ach, Sandy, more than ever before. And have you traveled far since last I saw you?"

"Ay, that have I, and many's the tale I'll tell you this day. But first I must show you something."

Beckoning Ian to his cart, Sandy pointed to a bundle wrapped up in his coat.

Tenderly unwrapping it, the old piper pulled out a young lamb, dirty, thin, and bleating.

"'Tis a poor hurt beastie, Ian," he said. "I found it on the road. Its mother is dead, and it was left to die, too. I picked it up and now cannot care for it, as I'm wandering and have no place to keep it."

"Ach, Sandy, couldn't I keep the wee beastie for you?" asked Ian eagerly.

Sandy stroked his chin thoughtfully.

"You could, laddie. But 't would be a while till I return—maybe not till next spring. And a lamb with no mother is a care."

"Ach, Sandy," cried the boy, "let me do it for you. I could feed it with my wee sister's nursing bottle."

"Ach, ay, laddie! Your mother would like that fine!" laughed Sandy. "But," he continued soberly, "if you would keep the wee creature, I could give you something for your trouble."

"No, Sandy. I would keep it for you, and gladly."

Sandy was still dubious. He was worried for fear the boy's father would object to a charge of this kind. The lamb would need tender nursing and careful watching.

Sometimes small boys grow careless, although their intentions are of the best. Then the task falls to Father or Mother.

As Sandy was revolving these thoughts in his mind, he suddenly had a plan.

"Ian," he said, "do you remember the story I told you of the pipers at Dunblane?"

"I've thought of little else, Sandy," replied Ian, as he stroked the lamb. The little creature was nestling down comfortably in Sandy's arms.

"Well, lad, uncover the plaid on my cart and see what I have there."

Ian turned back the bit of plaid covering the cart. Sandy used it to protect his personal belongings.

"Two sets o' pipes, Sandy!" exclaimed Ian.

"Ay! One was given me by a man for a service. It is not so bonny as mine but might do for a laddie learning to play!"

"Sandy, do you mean—?" Ian cried.

"Ay, lad. In the spring when I return, if this wee beastie is fine, and you have done your duty like a true shepherd, then you shall have the pipes!"

"Sandy, Sandy, is it true? May I be a piper and play the pipes like the laddies in Dunblane? Ach, Sandy!"

Ian was almost mad with joy. For a moment he forgot what service he was to render in return for this great reward. But remembering his charge, he carefully lifted the little lamb out of Sandy's arms.

He held it tenderly in his own, and said, "You'll find the wee beastie well and fat when you return in the spring, Sandy."

CHAPTER V

THROUGH SCOTLAND WITH SANDY

The warm air of spring was pleasant. The Craig family's supper was spread out before the door of their cottage. They ate outdoors so that they could enjoy the beauties of the evening.

It would not be dark here until very late. Ian's father could sit before his cottage door, reading his paper by daylight until almost eleven o'clock.

Now it was only seven. Mrs. Craig was ringing a bell, which echoed through the hills.

This was the way she called her husband and son to the evening meal.

Toward her came Ian, and some one was with him. Mrs. Craig strained her eyes to see, but she could not make out the stranger's figure.

As they came closer, Ian ran toward his mother, calling, "Mother, I've brought Sandy to tea!"

The old piper politely removed his cap and stood before Ian's mother.

"Your son has brought home an old traveler, mistress," he said.

Mrs. Craig smiled and, shaking Sandy's hand, said, "And glad I am, for a friend of Ian's is welcome to the house of his mother. Sit down, sir."

Ian told his mother the story of the lamb.

He explained how, if he performed his task, he would by next spring be the owner of bagpipes.

Mrs. Craig smiled at Sandy and said, "You trust the laddie, sir?"

Sandy MacGregor replied, "Ay; for will he not be a piper in the band one fine day?"

Alan Craig and Roy soon returned, and Sandy was introduced to them.

After the little repast, Ian beckoned Sandy to him. Nodding his head toward the hills, he said, "Come away and tell now about your travels through Scotland, Sandy."

The two sat on the hill and watched the smoke curling up from the cottage chimney. And while Sandy smoked his pipe he told Ian once more of his wondrous adventures.

Traveling through Scotland is like going through many different countries. For Scotland's beauties are varied. Here in the hollow is a lovely, quaint village. Its thatched roofs and white walled cottages make a picture sweet to behold.

As you go along, soon you pass the peaceful, hilly country and come to rocky, steep, and rugged land. You might be in the mountains, for it is wild and desolate except for the sheep, which are everywhere.

Around a corner, another village looms into space. This one is cold and bleak. You pass through it without sight or sound of human beings. Its buildings are tall, stony, and gray. In the center is a pump, where the people come to draw their water, but no one is about.

With a shiver you pass on. As you gradually leave the village behind, you find yourself again in pastoral land. Thatched cottages come into view. Bluebells begin to dot the road. How sweet is the smell of hay and cows and clover!

Once more a village, and now you wonder whether this can be the same country. For in the narrow streets are children, dogs, women, peasants, bicyclists, and more children.

Little girls walk along knitting. Everyone is walking in the middle of the cobbled street. Sandy has difficulty in going through the crowd with his cart.

This is Kurrimuir, better known as Thrums. It is the scene of many of J. M. Barrie's delightful stories. Here on the corner is the dear little cottage made famous by Barrie's "A Window in Thrums."

Passing a field, Sandy stops to watch some boys playing cricket. This game is very popular in Scotland. All the boys play it, just as American boys play baseball.

Doune Castle! Sandy climbs over the fence and starts up toward the towering mass of rock. He thinks of the many battles fought around this ancient stronghold. It was here that King Robert Bruce made some of Scotland's history.

Stirling Castle! Another massive stone memorial of the days of Scotland's stormy wars.

Sandy passes on until he comes to the city of Perth. Here he stops before the old, old house in which lived "The Fair Maid of Perth," made famous by Sir Walter Scott.

In St. Andrews is the oldest golf links in the world. From everywhere people come to play the royal and ancient game. It is said that no course is at all like the old course at St. Andrews.

As you perhaps know, golf originated in Scotland. St. Andrews is the place where it started. Some say that it was first begun by the shepherds. It is thought that they used to knock small stones with their crooks as they strolled behind their sheep.

On went Sandy to Melrose. He passed the Eildon Hills where King Arthur and his knights are supposed to be buried. This is the spot where, 'tis said, Sir Walter Scott used to stop his horses every day.

He paused here because he loved to look at the glorious view behind. His horses knew the spot so well that they would stop here of their own accord. On the day of Sir Walter's funeral, when they were taking his body to the Abbey, the horses stopped once more.

In Alloway is the house where the great Scotch poet, Robert Burns, lived. Every day it is shown to hundreds of visitors, who pay to go in and look at the curious old place.

Its quaint furniture and interesting manuscripts and pictures are all connected with the beloved poet. In the gardens are statues representing many of the characters in Burns' poems. "Poosie Nancy," "Tam O' Shanter," and many others are there.

Another town made famous by a Scottish character is Maxwelltown, or Maxwelton, where Annie Laurie lived.

Passing an ancient graveyard, Sandy stops to marvel at some huge slabs of iron. These are still kept to show how, in the seventeenth century, the dead were held down in their graves.

These heavy slabs were put on top of the dead. This was done to keep them from being dug up by robbers. The thieves would steal and sell them to doctors and medical students.

The signing of the Covenant was to Scotland what the signing of the Declaration of Independence was to America. It was the beginning of freedom!

James VI of Scotland tried to force the people into his own religious beliefs. They refused to be led. On the first day of March, 1768, in the Old Greyfriars Churchyard, the Covenant was signed.

The signing was done on a flat gravestone, which is there to this day. And so, just as America has a Liberty Bell, Scotland has a Liberty Stone.

As Sandy's old handcart rattles through each little Scottish town, he is impressed with the many bookshops he sees in his country. The Scotch are enthusiastic readers. Their love and desire for education are national traits.

Often Sandy passes young boys or young girls sitting by the roadside, absorbed in their books. The colleges and schools of Scotland are fine indeed.

When Sandy asks a direction, he is sure to receive a courteous reply. The children who come to his side are polite and kind and anxious to help. They will gladly do what they can for a stranger and do not ask any pay in return.

Over many stores and buildings Sandy reads names which start with "Mac," such as MacNiel and MacKenzie. He smiles as he thinks about these names. He knows that these people, like himself, are the descendants of the old clan leaders.

They gave the name "Mac," which means "son of," to their children. So, if a clan leader was named Gregor, the children of his clan would be MacGregor. In the olden days, the word "clan," which comes from an old Gaelic word meaning "children," was like a great family. Their chief was like a father, whom they all obeyed.

To-day, you no doubt know people named MacDonald, MacRae, etc. These are the descendants of the "clansmen," as they were called.

Each clan has a tartan of its own. A tartan is what you would probably call plaid. It is the heathery mixture of many colors and designs.

Each tartan is different from every other. To-day in Scotland you will see the children wearing kilts or ties or tams made of their own family tartan.

The town of Paisley is famous for its Paisley shawls. These are very much admired by all the world and worn by ladies of fashion.

The Shetland shawls, also famous, are dear to old ladies, because they are soft and warm. The Shetland ponies are dear to children, for they are so little that they are more like large dogs than like horses. Both come from the Shetland Islands, which are north of Scotland and are ruggedly wild.

Through all of Sandy's travels he never saw the thistle, which is supposed to grow so thickly in Scotland. The thistle, as you perhaps know, is used on Scottish crests and banners. No doubt it existed, long ago, but to-day it is nowhere to be found.

Here is Loch Drunkie, a queer name with a queer history. It was on the shores of this lake that men made whisky—which was against the law.

One day the men saw officers of the law coming toward them. They knew that they would be arrested if they were found out. To avoid arrest, they emptied their whisky into the lake. People say that the waters have remained half whisky from that day to this.

Sandy jogs along toward Aberfoyle. It is the day he delivers his injured lamb to the mercies of his young friend. During this time, he passes another "loch," the well known and much beloved "Loch Lomond."

Sandy stops on the shore. He gazes below on the shining blue waters, upon which ply the tiny white steamers. He shoulders his bagpipes and plays the melody known in every clime, "On the bonny, bonny banks of Loch Lomond." Here the fairies were wont to dwell. A tale is told of fairy dyers, who worked for the clans of Loch Lomond in the days of yore.

A joke was once played upon the wee elfin folk by a boy. The lad asked to have the fleece of a black sheep dyed white. Angered by this request, the fairies overturned their pots of dye into the lake and never more returned.

But the color from their dye turned the lake an unearthly shade of blue. This color is different from that of all other lakes, and thus it has remained.

Again Sandy pipes:

"For me and ma true love will never meet again

On the bonny, bonny banks of Loch Lomond."

CHAPTER VI

IAN'S BETTY

For many weeks after Sandy's departure from Aberfoyle, Ian tended the lamb carefully. He fed it from a baby's bottle. The young creature grew strong and fat. It would follow the boy around as though it knew him to be its nurse.

It was a loving little animal, and Ian became very fond of it. He would take it with him when he sat with his father upon the hill where Roy guarded the other sheep.

It did not mingle with the others, for it was an orphan. It knew that it did not belong with the flock. Sheep are not like people. Human beings, seeing a motherless child, would strive to protect it with their own young ones.

So the task of protector and nurse fell to Ian. He loved to feel the wee one's soft fur against his cheek as it lay on the hill with him. He liked to feed it from its bottle and hear the soft, gurgling noises it made.

It amused him to see its tail waggled so rapidly after each mouthful of milk. This is the way it showed Ian how well it liked its dinner. And as Ian felt the lamb, warm and soft in his arms, he seemed to feel there something else—his beloved bagpipes!

Much to the amusement of his parents, Ian called the lamb Betty, his baby sister's name. He felt that it was as helpless and young as she.

Very often they both sucked from their nursing bottles at the same time. While they were doing this, they looked at each other with big, wondering eyes. Ian often sat and admired the pair and laughingly said to his mother, "Your baby and my baby, Mother."

So the days flew by, and the summer wore on. Soon the school bell began to ring out again. It told the children that another term was beginning.

Ian was loth to leave his happy pastimes in field and on hill. However, he, like all Scotch children, was anxious to learn. So one morning, he strapped his book bag on his back and started off to school.

That was a lonely day for the lamb Betty. She was lonely because her young guardian had hardly ever left her side. The lamb was clearly worried and bleated unmercifully until Ian returned from school.

When, the next day, the same thing happened, Ian's pet could stand it no longer and started out to find him.

Every child in the world knows the song about "Mary's little lamb." That day, as Betty marched herself up the steps of Ian's schoolhouse, a chorus of childish voices sang out:

"Ian had a wee, wee lamb;

It followed him to school!"

There was much merriment as Ian hurriedly packed Betty off to her home. Like the teacher in the song, this teacher had difficulty in restoring order.

It was also a flushed and embarrassed Ian who returned to his classroom. That evening he lectured Betty upon behavior for lambs!

However, Betty was either disobedient or else too young to understand Ian's lecture. The next day she tried to repeat her performance. She started off on a gallop to find her young master. I say, "tried," for alas, this time poor Betty could not find Ian's school!

For many hours she wandered about. She went farther and farther, not only from school but from home. Evening fell, and Betty was bleating alone in a dense forest—lost!

At last Ian returned from school. For several moments, he could not understand why Betty did not come to meet him. He stood and gazed about. Then a terrible thought came to him.

LOST!

Rushing to his father on the hillside, he asked excitedly for his pet. Alan Craig shook his head sadly.

"I've sent Roy again, laddie, but he's returned once alone. I fear the beastie is lost."

Lost! Ian's world fell about him. The sound of distant bagpipes seemed to resound dully in his ears. The words of Sandy came to him through the dim: "In the spring, if this beastie is fine, and you have done your duty—"

His duty! And poor Betty! Where could she be? A little lonely creature, more baby than animal, tended so carefully, and unused to the thorns and sharp rocks of the hills—alone and lost!

"Father!" was all that Ian could gasp. Just then he saw Roy coming toward them, his tail between his legs. An expression of failure was in his shepherd eyes.

"Roy, lad, can you not find her?" asked Ian.

Ian threw his school books off his back. Kneeling, he put his arms around the neck of Roy. Roy answered in his own way. It was as clear to Ian as though the dog had cried out to him, "No, laddie, she's lost, lost!"

And if a sheep was lost to Roy, it was indeed a lost sheep! For the clever dog would smell a sheep for many miles. He would, in fact, encounter any danger to bring a straggler back to the fold.

Still, thought Ian, Betty was not really one of the fold. It was possible that Roy's experience did not fit him to scent out tame pets.

"I'm going to look, Father," shouted the heartbroken boy.

Calling Roy, he started off on a run. The father shook his head and felt a great pity for his little son.

CHAPTER VII

ALAN CRAIG TELLS A STORY

The word "Betty" resounded in the hills many times that evening. The lights in the village were already lighted when a tired, heartsick boy, followed by a sympathetic sheep dog, returned to the Craig cottage.

There they were awaited by Alan Craig. The lad stumbled blindly into the house.

He found his father with a candle in his hand, waiting to lead the disappointed boy to his bed.

Ian cried himself to sleep that night. Roy, the dog, sat beside him and mourned for the lost member of the little household.

The next day and the next were spent in searching the hills, the fields, and the forest. Fortunately for Ian, they were Saturday and Sunday, and he did not have to go to school.

He arose before the dawn and did not return until evening. But it was always the same. Betty was nowhere to be found. Though Ian and Roy hunted in every conceivable place, the lamb had disappeared.

On Monday, Ian was forced to relinquish his hunt and go to school. Immediately after school he called to Roy and was off again.

"The lad hardly eats his meals, he's so troubled!" said Mrs. Craig to her husband, as she shook her head.

Alan bit his pipe in silence, while his heart bled for Ian.

Alan had been training a new dog for the sheep. He was using this dog instead of Roy, who was allowed to stay with Ian and help him in his search.

But this meant added work for Alan, who had to be on the watch. He could not leave his charges completely in the care of this new helper, as he had done with Roy. Many times the new dog frightened the sheep. They soon became panicky and ran in all directions.

Then the dog forgot all of Alan's training and ran after them wildly. Alan always had to come himself to restore order.

One day he tramped miles to recover a terrified mother and her baby. After this long walk, Alan sat on the hillside.

Meanwhile the new dog looked at him out of the corner of his eye, and dropped his tail because he was ashamed.

As the shepherd sat smoking, he saw his son coming toward him, followed by Roy. Ian threw himself down beside his father. Letting his head sink upon the shepherd's knee, he gave up the search.

"'Tis weary I am, Father," he sighed. "The search is over, and my wee lamb is gone."

"And your pipes, Ian? Are they to be lost, too?" queried the shepherd.

"Ay," answered his son, "for Sandy said, 'If you tend the wee creature well till spring!' Now Sandy will return in the spring, and there'll be no creature."

For a few moments Alan Craig smoothed Ian's curly black hair. The boy tried hard to hold back his sobs, which were nearly choking him.

Then Alan Craig spoke. "Ian, lad, have you not heard the story of Bruce and the spider?"

"Ay, Father," replied Ian. "'Tis in my history book."

"Then mind well while I repeat it to you. For King Robert Bruce was a great man, and he never gave up!"

Ian listened intently while his father recounted the well-known tale. He told how, many, many years ago, King Robert Bruce had fought with the English and lost numerous battles. One night, he was lying despondent on a rude couch in his tent on the battlefield.

His heart was heavy with the memory of his lost battles and of the suffering throughout his country. Just then his eye fell upon a spider in the corner of the tent. The industrious little creature was trying to fix its web to the top pole of the tent. It had already made six attempts, but each time it had fallen.

King Bruce bethought him of his lost battles. Six! He and the spider had failed six times. And now he, King Bruce, was about to give up! Would the spider also be downed, or would it, perhaps, persevere once more?

King Bruce made a vow to himself. He decided that, should the wee creature try again to fix its web and be successful, then he, Robert Bruce, would profit by the spider's lesson and fight another battle!

The spider made another attempt. Slowly it raised its shadowy body until, quivering in the air, it balanced itself for the final plunge. The King raised himself on his elbow and watched. A nation awaited that spider's success or failure!

Again it plunged, caught at the pole, and fixed its web! King Robert Bruce jumped to his feet. He threw his plaid about him and began his preparations for the greatest battle in Scottish history, the Battle of Bannockburn.

As everyone knows, he routed the English at this famous battle. Never afterward would the great King give up!

"So should we all feel, Ian," said Alan Craig as he finished his tale.

"From the King to the spider!" Though Ian had heard the story often before, it now held a new meaning for him. He looked up at his father.

Then he stood erect and called to his dog, "Come, Roy; we'll try again!"

He was soon off through the hills once more.

CHAPTER VIII

PIPERS AND TROUBLES

At the beginning of that same summer, Jamie Robinson, Aberfoyle's piper, became restless. Jamie was not a steady man. He had never been a good provider. His poor wife and babies were often hungry and cold in the stormy winter months.

Jamie Robinson earned his living by his piping. He marched back and forth through the village street, playing his bagpipes. He hoped that the noisy, celebrating crowds, which arrived from Glasgow, would like his music and throw him pennies.

When the people were generous, his family might have a good dinner. But often Jamie Robinson did not bring the money home to his family. Unfortunately Jamie, who was a weak man, was often led by some of the village men into public houses. Here men gamble and drink.

Sometimes poor Mrs. Robinson waited until very late for her husband to come home. When at last he arrived, he came penniless.

But now Jamie was buoyed up by the balmy weather. He felt a longing for the open road.

"Come away, wife," he pleaded. "'Tis no living for a man here."

But Mrs. Robinson only shook her head and reminded him of their large family and of the hardships of a wandering life. After all, they were comfortable here, when Jamie brought home the pennies.

They had a little corner on a bright meadow beside a brook. Besides, the people of Aberfoyle were kind. Mrs. Robinson tried to keep her four wee children clean and happy. But this task was not always easy. What would it be on the open road?

"No, Jamie," she said. "'Tis afraid I am to go traveling with the wee bairns." (Children are called bairns in Scotland.)

But Jamie insisted and promised that she would not regret it. He promised that he would make money and provide for them better than before.

And so, one day the village of Aberfoyle said good-bye to Piper Robinson. The little caravan then moved on to what they hoped would be a better life.

They made a queer picture as they trudged along. There was Jamie pulling the cart, with Mrs. Robinson beside him. Her entire kitchen was strung upon her back—teakettle, sauce pan, and soup ladle.

Then came the oldest child, followed by the scrawny dog. Behind him dragged a freckled boy of five years. In the handcart, on top of the sticks and the tent, sat the two babies. One of them was three and the other barely two years old.

For some time Jamie Robinson was happy. In each little village where he played, he made enough to feed his family. He tried to please his wife and brought home all the money that was thrown him.

But the weeks wore on, and the family moved farther and farther from the big cities. Then it seemed that there became less and less money for pipers.

One night Jamie came back to his little brood with empty pockets. The rain had been falling all day. The family of Jamie Robinson had been huddled together in their tent like lost sheep. When Jamie entered the tent, the baby was crying. Jamie knew she was hungry.

While Sandy MacGregor traveled, he usually sang or whistled. Sandy was always happy. He was getting old, and his stride was not what it had been. Still he gloried in his happy-go-lucky life.

Since leaving Aberfoyle, Sandy had thought often of the little boy in whose charge he had left the baby lamb. Old Sandy chuckled to himself when he thought about his return and Ian's joy upon receiving the bagpipes.

"If I could only stay and teach the laddie to play!" mused the old piper.

Sandy was a good piper and had once served in the army. Jamie Robinson had only picked up a few tunes. Ian had recognized Sandy's clever playing at once on the day he had first come to Aberfoyle.

Now, wet from the showers and hungry, Sandy stopped in a town. Taking out his pipes, he began to play. It was the same town where Jamie Robinson had played that night and the night before. The people were poor.

The rain had been falling in steady showers, so that few persons were about the streets. Sandy puffed on his pipes, and the sweet melody echoed through the village and beyond to the hills. But not a soul came to pay the piper.

"Ach, well," sighed Sandy. He wiped the dripping water from his brow and put back the pipes. He covered them carefully with his plaid. Then pulling his cart, the old man moved on through the wet streets of the village. Soon he was on the open road.

His experienced eyes fell upon a camping spot. He decided to rest the night there. He neared the little clump of trees by the side of the road. Then he saw that he was not the only traveler who had chosen this spot. Here was the tent of Jamie Robinson.

As Sandy drew closer, he heard a baby crying. Sandy called out, and Jamie put his face out of his tent. A sullen, angry face it was.

"And what is it you want?" he bellowed.

Sandy walked up to the man and smiled.

"Ach, don't be angry," he said. "I'll not be harming you. I'm an old piper and would rest the night here beside you, if you have no objection."

Jamie looked at the cart and again at Sandy's happy red face.

Then, softening his tone, he said, "Then welcome. And have you piped to yon village?"

"Ay," answered Sandy, "but they have not cared for my music!"

He laughed as he said this, and started to pitch his tent.

Jamie came out and helped him. It was not long before he had told Sandy all of his troubles. Sandy's brows wrinkled. A sadness came over his face as he listened to Jamie's tale of woe.

The family had been stranded here for three days. The rain had kept them from moving. Then the wee baby was ill, and the others were hungry and cold. Not a penny had been made in the town. Jamie had played several times each day. He had even trudged along to the next town with no better results.

Sandy was shocked. The thought of hungry children tormented him. Telling Jamie that he wished to try his luck in the town once more, he hastened thither, his pipes under his arm.

Sandy had never been a rich man. He always had enough to buy his meals, and that was all. A piper cannot make a great deal. Sandy's music usually brought him ample money for his needs. But he was a generous soul and gave away half of what he earned.

To-night he had in his pocket just enough to buy his dinner. Into the town he went. It was not long before he returned to the suffering family with bread and milk. To Mrs. Robinson, Sandy appeared as a good fairy that night.

The next day broke fair. Early Sandy was in the market square of the town. He played the finest tunes he knew, strutting up and down.

The villagers liked his music, and the children followed him. They would have liked to shower Sandy with gold, for the joy that their country's melodies brought them. But their purses were thin. They could only smile sadly and shake their heads at the puffing old man.

There was nothing for the Robinsons to do but to move on. It was a difficult task for Mrs. Robinson. But with Sandy's help, she managed to pilot her little tribe along the muddy road to the next village.

For many days Sandy and the Robinsons traveled together. Sandy piped and gave them all he made, which was little enough. Often he himself would go hungry to bed.

It grew so bad that poor Sandy began to wonder what would happen to them. Not for worlds would he have left them. Never did such a thought enter his mind.

He worried more over the sick baby than did Jamie Robinson. Jamie was, in fact, to Sandy, another child. Sandy felt as though he had to protect the irresponsible piper along with his family.

These were terrible days for Sandy. He sold nearly everything he had to provide for the Robinsons and keep them from going hungry.

One day the baby became desperately ill. It needed a doctor. Sandy rushed to the nearest village. The doctor was brought and pronounced the baby in a serious condition. He said it must be given fresh milk and nourishing food. But to provide these things was too difficult for the little family.

One thought had been at the back of Sandy's mind all along. But he had not allowed himself to consider it seriously until now. This crisis, however, forced him to carry out a plan.

The bagpipes he had promised Ian were the only valuable possession in his little cart. They would bring enough money to save the baby's life.

Sandy pulled them out. He polished the silver and rubbed the chanter carefully to remove the dust. Meanwhile, his thoughts flew to Ian. In his heart he was used to calling Ian "the wee Scotch piper," for he hoped to see the boy realize his dream some day.

Now the pipes would have to go. He would have to return to the lad empty-handed and with his promise broken. Still, it was the only thing he could do. So poor Sandy sold the pipes.

Sandy returned from the village, with his pockets bulging. He seemed to see Ian in front of him, the wee lamb in his arms. Ian seemed to be looking expectantly and questioningly at his old friend.

And Sandy heard himself saying, "No, laddie. Sandy has disappointed you and has not brought you the pipes!"

CHAPTER IX

IAN TRIES AGAIN

Ian was once more in search of Betty. The story of King Bruce echoed in his ears and spurred him on. Roy, too, seemed to be inspired with new hope. He sniffed and ran, and ran and sniffed. Every once in a while, he would let out short, sharp barks.

"Do not weary yourself, lad," said Ian. "We have long to go this day, and we'll not give up."

With these words the boy began to whistle. A happiness seemed to come suddenly to him as though he already had Betty safe in his arms.

For many hours the boy and dog climbed and walked. At last they found themselves in a wild, rugged portion of the country, where Ian had never before been. Rocks were all about him. He descended into giant caverns.

He called, "Betty!" and received only an echo for reply. He went farther until it was so late that he could not think of returning home. He would surely lose his way in the darkness, if he attempted it. So he curled himself up between two massive rocks and, with Roy nestling close to his side, fell fast asleep.

At dawn, Ian was awakened by Roy. The dog was barking and making wild dashes in the direction of a large gulch near by.

He ran madly to the gulch, then dashed back again to Ian. His barks came in hysterical gasps.

Ian ran with Roy to the edge of the gulch. Looking down, the boy saw a terrible sight. Hanging on to a ragged ledge was a large mother sheep. It was one of his own father's, as he could see by the markings on the wool. The poor creature was bleating. A few feet above the ledge stood her baby lamb.

At each of Roy's barks, the mother sheep gave a little jump, and the ledge of rock quivered. Ian thought surely it would break and the sheep would be dashed to pieces on the rocks below.

"Down, down!" commanded Ian in the same voice as his father used to the dog.

Roy crouched and whined, but stopped his barking. Ian remembered that some of the mother sheep distrusted the dog. So it would be impossible for Roy to show himself now. What must be done must be done by Ian himself.

While the boy climbed down the precipitous rocks, the faithful dog, deprived of his rightful work, whined and howled. Had he not been trained to obey, he would never have stayed. But to a shepherd dog, a master's word is law.

Roy watched his young friend as the boy made the perilous descent to rescue the terrified animal on the ledge.

The sheep was large, and its wool weighed heavily. But Ian grasped the creature firmly. With all his might, he pulled until he had it on the rock above. When the baby lamb saw its mother coming, it uttered loud, joyous bleatings.

Ian could only think that the sheep had been led astray by his father's new dog. He was worried for fear that there were others which had strayed beyond. He decided to see, and started off beyond the rock hill.

But when Roy began to drive the mother sheep along, she became very angry. She ran at him with her head lowered. Roy could not manage her. She refused to obey him and Ian.

The boy, who carried a crook like his father's, was forced to resort to the only means of bringing her to order. With a quick sweep of the crook, he caught the baby sheep. He lifted it in his arms.

"Now, you'll come away," he said to the mother, as he walked on. Snorting, the mother sheep was forced to follow.

On and on walked Ian and Roy. And now the hunt was not only for Betty, but for more of his father's herd. Ian thought he would find some that might have been led astray by the new dog.

At noon he sat down to eat his "piece," which he carried in his sporran. When he had finished, he started for a clear stream near by.

As he approached, he thought he saw one of the grayish rocks in the stream moving. He rubbed his eyes. Could it be a reflection from the water? No. It was moving slowly.

Ian approached faster. What was his amazement at finding the gray rock to be his own Betty! It was his Betty, thin and ragged, and stumbling along on her front knees, too weak to raise her feet. Poor little beast!

She was nearly dead. As Ian raised her up, he realized that he had found her just in time. The creature seemed to know the boy, for she nestled down in his arms as of yore. In spite of her suffering, she seemed perfectly happy, now that her Ian was found.

CHAPTER X

SPRING

Spring! Each day found an eager, watchful boy, a happy, sweet-faced sheep dog, and a large fleecy lamb standing on the Rob Roy Brig. They were awaiting in glad anticipation a visitor, who was expected and whose music would soon reach the happy ears of a future piper.

Ian Craig had never allowed his Betty to roam after that frightful episode. She had been kept in a little corral, which Ian built for her. When he came home from school, he took her with him to the brig. He fastened her to a massive rock, while he awaited the return of Sandy.

Betty was now almost as fat and big as the other sheep. She was a credit to the boy's good care. So proud of her was Ian that he often tied a lovely tartan ribbon about her neck. He combed her wool tenderly each day before he started off for the brig.

Day after day, the two waited. Meanwhile, Roy looked on with kindly eyes, although he did not understand it all. Of course, Betty was equally ignorant of why she was made to pose with a floppy bow around her neck, tied to an annoying rock. But she was content, for Ian stayed beside her.

Sometimes as Ian watched and waited, he thought he heard the bagpipes in the distance. And as he heard, his heart beat faster. The moment of bliss when he could claim his reward, seemed to be upon him.

Then he often looked at Betty, and a qualm seized him. How could he part with the lamb? He had been through trouble and sorrow for the little animal. He had lived many happy hours by her side. It was as though she had become his own. The thought of parting from her was like a stab. Then, too, Betty loved him.

At these times, the poor little boy would knit his brow and ponder upon the strangeness of life.

Then he thought of the pipers and the tale of Dunblane, where the stalwart lads marched and played. He thought of the glorious piper bands marching in the big towns. The thought made him brighten and jump from the brig and scan the country for a sign of Sandy.

But the days of budding blossoms and showers in Scotland wore on. Finally Betty's ribbon bow began to fade and Ian's patience to wear.

Little Elsie Campbell used at times to walk with the boy to the brig. Often he stopped on the walk and talked to her, as he cocked his head on one side.

"Do you not hear the din of pipes, Elsie?" he asked.

And the wee lassie shook her head and said, "Ach, no, lad. 'Tis daft you are with your pipes!"

But it was said kindly, for Elsie hoped and prayed that Sandy would return. You see, Ian had told her the story of Betty and how he waited for the promised pipes. It was, in fact, Elsie who had first tied the silken tartan ribbon about the lamb's neck.

It was a gray day which promised rain. Ian and Betty neared the brig together. Ian had just tied the creature to her accustomed rock and was lifting himself to the wall when he heard a sound. Pipes! Unmistakably pipes!

Still, he had been mistaken so often before that he dared not look. And Elsie was not there to-day. She would have told him. For in her ears the sound was not always droning as it had been in Ian's for many days.

He had not told his mother for fear of worrying her. But his head was often heavy, and he could not sleep with the sound of the bagpipes. Poor little Ian! If only Sandy would return!

On this dull, misty day as he swung his feet from the wall of the brig, Ian could not stop the sound. Nearer and nearer it came!

Then, "Bonny laddie, Highland laddie," chanted the pipes. Ian looked up and saw standing before him his Sandy!

Although he was as red and wrinkled and twinkling as before, there was a change. Sandy was very shabby. His coat was stained with the mud and rain of many hard days.

He stopped his playing and stood before the boy. A sad, longing look came into his eyes.

"Ian, lad," he said slowly, "'tis Sandy come back."

And Ian suddenly realized that it was all true and not one of his dreams. He jumped down from the wall and threw his arms about Sandy.

"Ach, Sandy," he cried. Then he stood back and pointed to the lamb. Evidently Sandy had not noticed it.

"And do you not see our beastie, Sandy? 'Tis the same you left with me, and well and fat she is."

Sandy turned and looked at Betty. But he did not talk as Ian had expected him to, nor did he compliment Ian on the lamb's well-being. He only stood fingering his pipes and slowly shaking his head.

As Ian stared in wonderment, the piper lifted his bagpipes from his shoulder and handed them to the boy.

"Your pipes are here, lad, and Sandy keeps his promise!" he said.

Without thinking Ian put out his arms to receive the instrument. His eyes, however, did not leave his friend's face.

"But, Sandy, these are your own pipes you're giving me!" he said, as if he could hardly believe it, after looking down at what Sandy had placed in his arms.

"Ay, lad," answered Sandy, "and now you can be a fine piper, and Sandy himself will teach you to play."

Then Sandy told Ian the sad story of Jamie Robinson. He explained how he had sold nearly all his worldly goods to help the little family and put them on their feet again. He told of how he had left them comfortably settled near a prosperous village. He had made Jamie promise to work and save for his little brood.

Sandy also told how he had come all the way to keep his promise to the boy. He said, too, that now, as in Aberfoyle there was no piper, he expected to stay here and take Jamie Robinson's place if Ian would lend him his pipes each day for awhile. And in return, he would teach the lad to play!

"For I'm not so young as I was, laddie, and the wandering life is over for me," he added.

When Ian heard these plans, he was beside himself with joy. He hugged first Sandy, then Roy, and then Betty. At last the piper became his old jolly self once more and laughed.

"Ay, lad, we'll share the pipes together, though they belong to you. But old Sandy will have to make a living, and he'll teach you all the tunes he knows!"

No happier boy than Ian Craig lived in Scotland that night. Standing before the door of the cottage, he puffed and blew on his pipes. There issued forth the sound of a thousand sheep all bleating at once but all in pain! Sandy listened from his tent on the hill opposite and chuckled to himself.

Roy was also in pain as he listened. His delicate ears were unused to this shrieking and squealing. He joined in the din with loud howls.

The baby within the house was in sympathy, too, and added her wails.

So Sandy's first evening as a resident in Aberfoyle was not a quiet one. He was forced to stop his ears.

Mrs. Craig was unable to stand the racket. So she pulled her puffing son into the house and packed him off to bed, to the great relief of all.

But Ian was a quick and hard-working pupil. It was not long before Roy quite approved of the sounds his master made on his pipes. He did not then feel it necessary to amend the melody.

Also the baby gurgled with glee. She puffed out her cheeks in imitation of Ian and laughed happily. And Betty, the lamb, too, seemed to know that all was well. The world was in tune with the wee Scotch piper who had, at last, realized his dreams.

"'Tis the close of the day
At the foot of the ben,
And the sound of his pipes
Echoes back through the glen."

CHAPTER XI

THE WEE SCOTCH PIPER

It was a cloudless day in the big Scotch city. The people seemed to feel that something unusual was about to happen. Everyone wore his best, and the city fairly shone with the reds and blues and greens of tartan kilts and bonnets.

Soldiers paraded the streets. Children hurried along by their parents' sides, anxious to arrive at the big grand stand in time. Numerous bystanders flanked the wide street.

All the people were breathless with excitement. Even the usual crowding traffic suspended its pushing and shrill tooting. For this was a great day in Scotland. Many celebrations occur at intervals in this land of excursions and picnics. But to-day was as the children would say, "extra special."

The huge grand stand was overcrowded with eager Scotchmen, with their wives and bairns. They all strained their eyes for a glimpse of the great "kiltie band," which was to march down the street.

Among those who watched, and perhaps the most eager of all, were a family of country folk. In bobbing black bonnet sat a calm-faced old lady. Beside her was a rugged old man. Both were in their best array. Both were longing for the sight they had come miles from their little farm to see.

The couple were none other than Alan Craig and his wife. The sight that their old eyes would soon see, as the happy tears dimmed their view, would be their son, their Ian. He was now a tall, manly piper in kilted uniform, marching and piping with the flower of Scotland's army.

By their side sat another. His kindly face shone with pride, and in his heart was a singing joy.

For Sandy MacGregor had taught this lad to play. It was the same old pipes of Sandy MacGregor that he still used. He would soon show those pipes to a cheering crowd as his fingers flew over the chanter. While he played, his arm would shelter the tartan bellows once sheltered by Sandy's own arm as the old piper had wandered over hill and through dale.

Sandy MacGregor had lived many years for this moment. As he craned his neck for a sight of the coming parade, he spoke to the little girl beside him.

"See, Betty, 'tis they coming now."

Betty, Ian's baby sister, was now a girl of the age Ian had been when first Sandy had met him.

Together, Betty and Sandy had dreamed and planned the day when together they would view their piper laddie on parade.

For Sandy had dwelt in the village of Aberfoyle these many years. While he had piped for his living, he had taught another piper, who was now to cover his old teacher with glory.

In the large audience there was still another, whose blue eyes danced with joy. Her hands were clasped together with excitement as she awaited the approach of her boyhood friend. It was little Elsie Campbell, now grown to womanhood. Elsie was among those who thrilled to see the "wee Scotch piper," as he marched along that day.

Who knows with what feelings of pride the lad looked up as he passed that grand stand? Who knows his feelings of love, on seeing those dear faces smiling and nodding at him?

And as he marched and played, he seemed to see before him a little schoolboy marching and playing. That boy was himself, trudging the streets of a wee village, followed by a bleating lamb!